Max's World

Steve Elliott
2016

For Nicola

—{ m }—

About Max

Max is a small boy who likes to feed ducks.

He is a constant source of happiness to his hard working mum

Here are just a few short stories about Max, his mum and all his friends in Max's world.

Index of
Max's Stories

Max and the Seven

What happened at nursery today?' asked mum, as they pulled away in the car.

I was seven said Max.

Seven? asked mum.

And so was the new boy who smells of cabbage said Max. We were pretending we had to save the village from the Mexican bandits.

Oh, the magnificent seven, said mum.

I think so said Max, Ginger and her friend with the long black hair that keeps a mirror in her pocket were playing too.

Were they the villagers? asked mum.

Ginger ate an apple and fell asleep. Cabbage Boy tried to kiss her but she said he wasn't charming, he was Droopy, said Max.

Did you kiss her? asked mum.

Na - I wasn't charming either. I was Yule Grinner said Max. Then that funny girl said mirror, mirror in my hand, who is the fairest in the land? and Ginger said Cabbage Boy!

What happened next? asked mum.

We all had to march about singing Hi Ho Hi Ho it's off to work we go, and then whistle said Max.

And from the back of the car came the tune from... The good, the bad and the ugly!

─────{ m }─────

Max and the Bread House

At the end of another long day at the hospital. Mum picked up Max from the nursery. As she strapped him in his car seat the she waited for the best bit of the day - hearing how his day had been.

What happened today Max? mum asked, as she started the car.

I was handsome! said Max.

You are handsome said mum.

No, said Max, I was handsome, and that new boy was kettle. The new boy who smells of cabbage. The one I told you about yesterday, remember?

Yes, said mum, you were handsome and the new boy was kettle.

That's right, we was pretending! Only kettle kept getting lost in the forest. I used a skipping rope to make a lead for him! And the handles made a good plug, added Max.

OK, so you're handsome and he's kettle with a lead, said mum, getting a little worried.

Yes, and we was in the forest and we came to a house. It was the wendy house outside in the playground but we was still pretending, continued Max.

OK, so you're in the forest with kettle and you reach a house? said mum.

Yes, said Max, but it had a girl in it.... yuck! She said she would only come out if me and Kettle would eat the house. And she was Ginger too!

What did you do? asked mum.

This is the clever bit, said Max, we pretended it was made of bread. But really it's plastic.

So, said mum, Handsome and Kettle got lost in the Forest and ate Ginger's bread house?

Yes said Max.

Max, said mum, what did you do with the plug on Kettle's lead?

Erm ... I got in a bit of trouble with that said Max!

Max and the Marmalade

Max, we are going to the beach today, said mum.

Wow said Max, can we take sandwiches?

Yes said mum, what would you like in them? she asked.

Marmalade and fish paste said Max, 50:50, you know that's means half and half.

I know 50:50 is half and half, but marmalade and fish paste? checked mum.

Yes said Max, I saw a book with a story about a little marmalade that lives in the sea. She was half a person and half a fish. If I take my net, I can use the sandwiches as bait and I might catch her, he added.

How about cheese and a penguin biscuit? asked mum.

Don't be silly said Max, penguins are only good for catching polar bears. Can we go to the shops on the way then? I've seen boxes of marmalade food there it's got her name on it said Max.

What's that then? asked mum.

Ariel, of course said Max!

—{ m }—

Max and Evolution

One day when Max had been having cuddle time with mum, Max said, mum, when you was little in the olden days did you have them funny clothes?

Like the flared trousers and platform shoes from the 70's we saw on the television? asked mum.

No they had big collars, said Max.

They had big collars too in the 70's said mum.

No, said Max, there was a Queen Lizbeth!

Don't get frustrated with me. There was a Queen Elizabeth in the 70's and I wasn't even born then said mum, getting annoyed.

There was a man called shoespear, said Max.

Ah, said mum, you mean Queen Elizabeth the first and Shakespeare. Those big collars are called ruffs.

Yes, well when grandad was little, before that, everyone wore armour, said Max. And before that, he said confidently, everyone was monkeys!

—{ m }—

Frank, the New boy at Nursery

We had a new boy start today' said Max all excited.

What's his name?' mum asked.

Well, Max said, his name is Stan but he's so cool he tells everybody to call him Frank. You wouldn't understand. It's a Jazz thing!

Whys that? asked mum.

Frank said that *Now, the end is near and he has to face the final curtain* said Max.

That's strange, replied mum, do you think Frank will be a new friend?

He did say *My friend, I'll say it clear; I'll state my case of which I'm certain.*

That is very strange, said mum, where is Frank from?' she added.

Frank said *He's lived a life that's full and travelled each and every highway* I think said Max looking a bit confused.

And more, much more than this, I did it my way, sang mum to herself.

Did he say if he had any regrets about leaving his old nursery? asked mum.

Regrets, said Max, *He had a few, but then again, too few to mention.*

What did he do there? asked mum.

He did what he had to do, he saw it through without exemption, said Max, *he planned each charted course, each careful step along the highway,* he added, struggling with the bigger words.

Did he have anything else to say Max?

More, much more than this, said Max.

And how did he do all those things? mum asked.

He did it his way! said Max. Then added, I told you he was so cool! I

[In memory of Stan Britt, amongst other things an author and aficionado of Frank Sinatra.]

Max, Ginger and a Film About Trains

Max was explaining to Ginger that shopping was not a sport, when Ginger said, you like trains don't you?

Yes said Max, 'specially steam trains.

My mum and dad had a film on the TV yesterday but it broke it, said Ginger.

It did? - How? asked Max.

Yes, it had no colour! It was busted properly, she said.

Oh, said Max, but what's that got to do with trains?

It had lots of 'em, all steam trains, said Ginger, but they was all in white and grey and black, she added.

Wow. Was Bob the Builder in it? asked Max.

Nah, said Ginger, it had a man who kept bumping into a lady at a train station and I think they were worried they didn't have much time to count up all their Easter Eggs.

Why's that? asked Max.

It was called Brief Egg Counter, said Ginger.

Oh, said Max, what happened?

Tea and buns mostly, said Ginger.

—————{ m }—————

Max and the Frog Prince

Max had a big smile as mum strapped him in the car to go home from nursery.

What are you smiling about? asked mum.

Ginger kissed me today he said.

Why was that? asked mum.

She said I was a frog! And if she kissed me I would turn into a real prince, said Max.

But you are already a real boy, replied mum.

But I was pretending to be Yoda! He's green and a bit like a frog, said Max, still smiling.

What happened next? asked mum.

Then Stan went all Han Solo, whoever that is. And Cabbage Boy ran around shouting Fruitini… Fruitini… '

Did she use the Force on you? asked mum.

She sat on me! said Max.

What did you say? mum asked.

With me… Always… That Kiss will be …..

I've got a very bad feeling about this, said mum to herself, have you turned into a prince? she asked aloud.

No, said Max, but I find your lack of faith disturbing… he added from the back of the car.

—{ m }—

13

Max
the Hood

What did you do today Max? asked mum.

I was Robin, Max said.

Who was Batman? asked mum.

No, not Robin, I was robbin' Robin' said Max.

Who's Robin Robin? asked mum.

Not Robin Robin, said Max getting cross, 'robbin the rich!

To give to the poor? asked mum.

Yes, said Max, Ginger was Little John and Cabbage Boy was Marion.

Oh, said mum, did you all dress up?

Yep, Cabbage Marion put one of his mum's old dresses on and I had to wear tights.

Really? said mum.

Yes, so no one would know it was me doing the robbin' laughed Max.

————{ m }————

Max
the Viking

Mum, I'm Thor, said Max.

The Viking? asked mum.

I'm not sure, said Max, looking a bit confused. Do you know where Avalon is? he added.

Avalon? asked mum, wrinkling her brow, I think that's where King Arthur went. The Vikings all go to Valhalla.

Max looked even more confused. And said, but I'm Thor!

Yes, said mum, Thor, one of the Viking gods. We saw him on the TV yesterday.

But I'm Thor here, said Max pointing at his knee, I fell over and banged it up bad. I need to get Avalon.

Mum looked blank.

White cream, in the blue tube! exclaimed Max.

Oh - Savlon! said mum

—————{ m }—————

Max and the Secret Goodies Ring

It was Saturday and Max was pretending to be a policeman.

Excuse me mum, could I look in your bag? enquired Max.

Sure, what are you looking for? asked mum.

The facts mum, just the facts! What do we have here? Some red wine, Marks and Sparks meal deal for 2, veggie pasta bake and a packet of ginger biscuits. Nothing out of place here!

But Max had seen the secret pocket in the bag – and in it were the goodies!

Is there a problem Max? asked mum.

I've got reports that there is a secret goodies ring in the area!

Really? said mum.

Yes, apparently the ring leader is a lady who goes by the name grandma. But we don't know who her supplier is.

Oh, said mum, as she reached for her red coat, are you ready to go? she added.

Yes, said Max, where are we going?

To grandma's house, said mum.

Mmm, thought Max, finally a break in the case. I better make sure I get all the facts.

Why Max, what big ears you're getting, said mum, as she put his woolly hat on.

All the better to hear the facts mum, he said, why are we going to grandma's house?

She's not well and stuck in bed today, said mum.

Mmm, thought Max. That's a nice red coat' he said, is it new?

No, said mum, I wear it every time I go to see grandma.

Max had a report that grandma's supplier may be a lady in a red coat.

Hi grandma, called out mum as they let themselves into her house, are you still in bed?'

Yes dear, came a voice from upstairs, have you got something nice for me?'said the voice, send Max on up.

Max dropped his coat on the floor and ran on up the stairs. A few minutes later mum appeared in grandma's room with a big plate of goodies to share.

Max, try one if these, she said.

Thanks mum, said Max.

Why Max, what big teeth you're getting, said grandma.

All the better to taste the facts grandma! said Max.

Well, you're certainly wolfing that down! said mum and grandma together. Would you like another?

The Max Files

So the Jaffa Cakes where on the table. And now they are gone?

Yep, said Cabbage Boy.

So aliens did it? asked Max.

Yep, said Cabbage Boy.

So aliens flew all the way here to take Cabbage Boy's Jaffas? asked Ginger.

Yes, said Max, eating a sponge biscuit covered in chocolate with an orange jelly centre.

Really?'asked Ginger again, amazed.

Yes, well perhaps the laws of physics means on their planet you can't make the sponge or the jelly or the chocolate, said Max, taking another from the box in his pocket.

But they were here before you walked in, said Cabbage Boy.

They must have a Jaffa-porter to beam them up, explained Max.

Really? said Ginger again, I suppose the truth is out there ... she said.

Mumph ... said Max tucking into another one.

{ m }

Max the
Pasty Miner

The pasty mines of Cornwall are all closed now, said Max, but in the olden days there was lots of them. I read it in a book.

No said Cabbage Boy, they catch pasties out at sea with boats called trawlers.

That's fish fingers, said Max knowingly. And, he continued, there are still lots of deep Cornish mines that could be opened back up as soon as pasty prices get high enough.

When the mines where open, they had big steam engines to lift the pasties up the shafts, that's the traditional way. But they have new electric mines now for the jam and cream seams and the scones.'

Oh, said Cabbage Boy, but I only asked if you had seen my pasty that was for my lunch.

Mmmm unch, said Max with his mouth full.

The Max-kateer

Max came running into the kitchen shouting - On Guard!

Are you a musketeer today? mum asked.

Oui, said Max. He had a large disk of cardboard with a hole cut in it so it fitted on his head like a large floppy hat, and in one hand he had a sword made of straws.

Touché! said mum.

Bless you! said Max, and offered her a hanky in a very flamboyant way.

Why monsieur, with this hanky you are really spoiling me. That reminds me we have to go to the shops, she added, the chocolates are on special.

Are they 2 for 1 or 1 for 2?' said Max ...

The Three Max-kateers

Max enjoyed being a musketeer so much he played it with Cabbage Boy and Ginger when they came over for tea. Three Max-keteers was enough, considering the size of their floppy hats and spiky swords made of straws.

So after much 'on guard-ing' and 'touché-ing' and many swashbuckling adventures, tea was ready.

Here's tea, called mum.

Is that all for one? the Max-keteers said together.

No' said mum, it's to share!

———{ m }———

Max the Penguin

Skipper! said Ginger.

Yes Private, said Max, what is it?

Do we have to be penguins?

Yes, said Max, and he added,well boys, looks like we have a job to do, our friends are in danger. Captain's log, Private write this down! We are going to be working in a hostile environment.

Kowaski, that's you Cabbage Boy, we need to win the hearts and minds of the natives.

Reco, that's you Stan, we need some special tactical equipment we are going to face extreme peril. Before we go in I just want to say it's been a real pleasure serving with you boys.

But Max ...

Sorry Skipper, it's a surprise nursery nit check! We need a plan, whispered Ginger, as they stood in the queue.

No problem, said Max, smile and wave boys, smile and wave!

And after a bit more thought he added, Private Ginger might not survive!

—————{ m }—————

Max and the Rain

Max does not like the rain. He loves it! Like small boys everywhere it makes him grumpy, ill-tempered and generally not nice if he is forced to stay in out of it.

Today it was raining! When he woke he could hear it raining on the window. He got up quietly, found his blue suit and red wellington boots. He put them on and got back in to bed to wait for mum. Today was Saturday and they always fed the ducks on Saturday and he wanted to make sure that his mum would stick to the plan.

Max could not tell the time yet but he had a clock in his room and both hands pointed straight up... so he knew it wouldn't be long!

{ m }

Max, Stan and Casablanca

Stan sat at the nursery piano.

Go ahead Stan, she said, play it for me.

Stan closed his eyes he knew when trouble was coming ... plink, plink, plink...

You must remember this. A kiss is just a kiss. A sigh is just a .... dumm de dumm, ...as time goes by.... He sang badly, and he never did know all the words.

You must remember this a kiss is .... repeated Stan again, just as badly.

Just then Max walked up to Stan and placed a hand on Stan's shoulder. He said, I told you never to play that song again!

But boss, said Stan, 'she's ... '

Hello Max, she said, stepping away from the shadow of the Wendy House.

Stan felt Max's grip tighten slightly then Max turned to face her. He remembered how she looked, and she looked like he had been remembering in black and white.

Of all the Wendy joints in this nursery she had to walk into mine, he said, and you can stop singing Stan, he added.

Aren't you pleased to see me? she asked.

I'm saying this because it's true. Inside of us, we both know you don't belong with me, he replied. If that plane leaves the ground and you're not on it you'll regret it. Maybe not today. Maybe not tomorrow, but soon and for the rest of your life' he whispered.

But what about us? she asked.

We'll always have The Wendy House, he replied.

But when I said I would never leave you... she started.

And you never will, said Max, but I've got a job to do. Where I'm going, you can't follow. What I've got to do, you can't be any part of. I'm no good at being noble, but it doesn't take much to see that the problems of three little people don't amount to a hill of beans in this crazy world. Someday you'll understand that!

Max placed his hand under her chin and raised it so their eyes met.

Here's looking at you kid, he said, play it again Stan.

You must remember this ... sang Stan.

The
A-Max

Cabbage boy, said Max, put these necklaces on. And when I say **now**, say the words I told you.

Then Max spoke In his best army style voice ...

"In 2014 a crack toddler team were sent to the naughty step by a nursery court for a crime they did not commit. These toddlers promptly escaped from a maximum security Wendy House to the playground.

Today, still wanted for looking cute, they survive as toddlers of fortune. If you have a problem and no one else can help. If you can find them may be you can hire the Max team!"

Dum dee dum, dum dum dum, sang Ginger.

Now Cabbage Boy, said Max.

Cabbage Boy looked up sighed and said, what you talking about fool?

I love it when a plan comes together, chuckled Max.

The
Max-Factor

OK, now we are going to vote, said Max. Cabbage Boy what's your vote?

I say yes, said Cabbage Boy.

You have said yes to everything, said Max, what about you, Ginger?

I vote absolutely yes, she said.

OK, mum, he called from the kitchen table, we will have a cheese sandwich and a glass of juice each, said Max.

Will you? said mum, waiting for the magic word from her son.

Yes, you got three yes's said Max, what are you making for the next round?

—{ m }—

Max and the
3 Little Pigs

Well, said Cabbage Boy, Stan was the wolf and Ginger was one of the little pigs.

And? asked Max.

Ginger took the bank into the Wendy House like you said she would, said Cabbage Boy.

So the piggy bank was in the house? asked Max.

Yes, replied Cabbage Boy, then Stan said he would huff and he would puff and he would blow the house in.

And? asked Max

Well Stan huffed and he puffed and the Wendy House... fell in!

But... started Max, all I said was blow the bloody doors off!

Max and
the Alarm

Mum, did you know that in South Mercia they have special animals that keep burglars out? asked Max.

Really? said mum.

Yes, said Max, they have at least two types.

They do? said mum, astounded, are they some sort of dog?

No, they look like sheep with long legs, or short camels with no 'umps, he said.

Max continued, yes there is a house lama and a car lama. And they even have a special one for that shop on the corner.

They do? asked mum.

Yes, the deli lama! said Max.

—— { m } ——

007
Max

Cabbage Boy walked into the Wendy House with a toy white cat he had found in the toy box.

Well, Mr Bond we meet again, he said.

Do you expect me to talk Dr Cabbage? asked Max, struggling with the tinsel that tied him down.

No.... I expect you to cry, said Cabbage Boy, stroking his cat, but first Ginger is going to kiss you.

Yuck, said Max.

OK I'll do it then, said Dr Cabbage reaching for the mistletoe.

OK, said Max, I know about your plan.

Mr Tiddles, said Dr Cabbage to his cat, he knows about our plan.

I know you and Ginger are going to steal Big Reds wheels! You're going to make his deliveries, but to all your mates on The List!

What List? said Dr Cabbage, reaching for a mince pie, and putting down his cat.

The List! said Max.

The Naughty List? asked Dr Cabbage, tightening his big black belt and pulling up his red hood.

Max looked very worried as Ginger walked in. She put on a hat with two coat hangers stuck to it.

Excellent, Dr Cabbage said to her, now put on that red nose. Remember! Tis the night before Christmas, and all through the house not a creature is stirring, not even a mouse, sadly for Mr Tiddles, said Dr Cabbage picking up his cat and fixing it to his face.

But you wouldn't want a visit from Santa this year? Ho Ho Ho!

Max's Christmas

It was Christmas Eve and Max knew, as he pretended to fall asleep, that his mum would slowly back out of his room and close the door.

As he expected, a few seconds later there was the tapping. He was up and out of bed fast and over to the window and pulled back the curtains. On the other side of the glass was just what Max was expecting - the skipper of the crack commando penguins from the zoo.

Max, he said, we have a mission and we need your help.

Max pulled on his red wellies and his blue waterproof suit over his pj's and and climbed out the window. What is it? he asked.

This fella in the red coat is code named Santa cos that's his ... um ... name, one of his reindeer has gone rogue and defected to the fairy side. But that's not the worst of it, said skipper, it's red himself.

Not Rudolf? cried Max ... holy sleigh bells! he added.

The one and only, said skipper.

But, the fairy side? asked Max.

The Tooth Fairy! said skipper. She's a Jedi! Thats how she gets the teeth out.

That explains a few things, thought Max ,rubbing his jaw.

But she's more machine than fairy now, added skipper. When Rudie Redski leads out the sleigh, he's going to lead them straight to her star.

But there is still good in him, said Max, I can sense it...

Fruitini! said skipper, you're talking canned fruit, that force mumbo jumbo won't help us now. We need a plan!

Later, hiding in the smuggling compartment with the penguins on Santa's sleigh heading straight for the fairy star, Max thought - I have a bad feeling about this. Fairy stood on the flight deck of her star as the sleigh was tractored on board. She felt a disturbance that she had not felt for some time.

Search that ship, she commanded, I want to know what you find.

But Max, skipper, Santa and the team had already slipped aboard. The plan had seemed simple enough - hide in the sleigh until they get to the fairy star and rescue the princess (Max had forgotten when she was made part of the plan). Santa was going to fix the tractor beam and then they all had to "get the hell out of there with or without comrade Rudie the Redski!" as skipper put it.

All had gone to plan and, as they met back on the flight deck with the princess, Rudie and Santa, Fairy stepped from the shadows of the sleigh.

I've been waiting for you Santa,she said.

Holy Christmas Angels! said skipper.

When we last met I was but the apprentice. Now I am the master, said Fairy.

Yes Fairy, but you still can't go on top of the tree, laughed Santa.

But I know what you have for Christmas - I felt your presents', whispered Fairy ...

Max and the Stars

Who's that on the TV? asked Max.

It's Brian Cox, said mum, he's a professor, she added.

Wow, Max said, I've seen him on TV before talking about periscopes.

Periscopes? asked mum.

Yes, for fish and crabs and stuff.

Like you find at the bottom of the sea when you go in a submarine? mum asked, confused.

No like you get in the stars with horses! said Max.

Oh horoscopes! said mum, what did he say?

Things can only get better!!!

{ m }

The Hairy
Dog-Father

O n guard! said Cabbage Boy.

Touché away! said Max, as the pair faced one another on the school path.

But I don't believe it! said Cabbage Boy.

Max was pretending. He wasn't sure exactly what as, but he had a black cape and a mask on.

Search your feelings, said Max, I am your hairy dog-father ... don't underestimate the power of the force ... you shall go to the ball Cabbage Boy ...!

Max
the Pirate

Sail ho! .... a Spanish ship on the starboard bow cap'n, said mum.
Arrrrrr Spandinards? That she be! said Max, steady as she goes
first mate, he added.

Aye cap'n, said mum.

Arrrrrrr, this is the fastest sailing sofa in the whole Caribbean, said
Max, they looks to be just a bunch of landlubbers!

Aye, said mum.

Make your heading south south west, said Max. We'll take her over
the shallows of dining table reef - that's made of solid oak, that will
rip the bottom rite out them Spandinards!

Aye cap'n, but ... started mum.

Don't you be fretting lad, said Max, we'll soon make port. There'll
be plenty of scumpet and wenching for ye!

Scumpet and wenching? asked mum.

Aye, said Max looking a bit embarrassed. Scrumpets go in the
toaster and you puts butter on them.

And wenching? asked mum.

Wenching is a kind of .... um .... like a spanner, said Max, for putting the butter on.

Arrrrr, said mum, scrumpets it is then.

Shiver me timbers. Let's give these Spandinards a message where the sun don't shine, said Max, run out the cannons, run up the periscope and dive the boat ...

Aye cap'n, said mum, dive, dive, dive! she added.

Let's torpedo them right in the poop deck! said Max enthusiastically.

Arrrr cap'n, all hands on deck! yelled mum.

Max and the Nativity

Mum you have to come to the school next week, I'm in the nativity, Max said in rapid fire excitement.

You are? asked mum, who are you going to be? A wise man or a shepherd? she added, secretly hoping it was Joseph.

I wanted to be the donkey, said Max.

The donkey? sighed mum.

Yep, said Max, but we are not having one so I'm going to be Joseph, he said in a disappointed tone.

Yes! said mum, punching the air.

No! I have to hold the little baby Jesus, said Max.

Is Ginger going to be Mary? asked mum.

Na! Cabbage Boy is doing it - Ginger is a shepherd. I was thinking he was more wise man material myself, said Max, but apparently he likes to dress as a girl. I told him no kissing in the manger, not like last time!

Like last time? asked mum.

—— { m } ——

Max's
Valentine Card

One day when mum was emptying Max's school bag she found a card.

What's this? she asked.

It's a valentine's card, said Max.

And that is what it was. A folded blue card with a big pink heart stuck on the front. It was covered in glitter and stick on stars.

Max, said mum, you are supposed to give this to someone you like.

Are you? he said.

Yes, said mum.

Oh, he said, but it's got a poem inside can you read it?

Now Max is not known for his poems so, with some hesitation, mum got down on the floor so they could read it together.

On this valentine's day
I would like to take the time to say
As time goes on and I grow up
I may fall in love with pretty girls
Spend time with smart girls
And laugh with some girls that are funny
But you, my mummy will always be my best girl xxx

With tears in her eyes mum put her arms around her son and gave him a big hug. Max knew what to do to. He put his arms gently around his mum's neck and whispered in her ear.

Mum?

Yes Max? she said.

Can I have a biscuit?

Max and the Easter Eggs

It's Easter, said mum.

Egg-xactly! said Max.

I have 3 eggs, said max ,all chocolate ,he added. One's as big as my head, he said eggcitedly....

An egg-straviganzar! said mum.

How many do you have mum? Max asked.

Just one, she said.

Oh, said Max, would you like one of mine?

No, but thank you it's fine. One is just fine for me, she said smiling...

it's an egg-xtra large one she added!

—————{ m }—————

Mother's Day
with Max

Mum woke early. All was quiet. She knew Max had been planning something for Mother's Day, But just what was still a mystery?

It was, of course, a secret, but Max was not good at secrets. He kept saying "I've got a secret mum but I can't tell you" which was a bit of a giveaway.

So just what was going to happen?

He wasn't waiting at the foot of the bed with a tray of tea and toast soaked in tea. Nor was he outside the door waiting with a glass of orange juice... on the carpet.

Then, from the kitchen, Max called, I'm in here mum.

With a mounting sense of Mother's Day dread, mum walked towards the door and, as she did, she could hear, don't go into the light! But what she found was no tea, no tea toast and no OJ carpet.

On the table was ... a card and Max sat with the biggest of smiles! Mum gave Max a big hug relieved that there was no Mother's Day cleaning up to do!

Now, Max said - I'm going to make breakfast!!!

Many thanks to
Susanne - not only my
friend, but also my
editor.

———{ m }———

Printed in Great Britain
by Amazon

26112987R00027